**CTW**

## SESAME STREET®

# Oscar's New Neighbor

By Teddy Slater Margulies
Illustrated by Lauren Attinello

## A SESAME STREET/GOLDEN PRESS BOOK

Published by Western Publishing Company, Inc.,
in conjunction with Children's Television Workshop.

© 1992 Children's Television Workshop. Sesame Street puppet characters
© 1992 Jim Henson Productions, Inc. All rights reserved. Printed in the U.S.A. No part of this book may be reproduced or copied in any form without written permission from the publisher. Sesame Street and the Sesame Street sign are registered trademarks and service marks of Children's Television Workshop. All other trademarks are the property of Western Publishing Company, Inc. Library of Congress Catalog Card Number: 91-77259 ISBN: 0-307-00128-8   MCMXCIII

This educational book was created in cooperation with the Children's Television Workshop, producers of SESAME STREET. Children do not have to watch the television show to benefit from this book. Workshop revenues from this product will be used to help support CTW educational projects.

Early one morning Oscar the Grouch woke up to the sound of honking horns. He poked his head out of his trash can to see what was going on. A big moving van was blocking Sesame Street.

"Heh-heh-heh!" said Oscar. "What a great traffic jam! It'll be hours before they get *this* mess straightened out."

Oscar couldn't help smiling as he watched the movers unload a beat-up trash can.

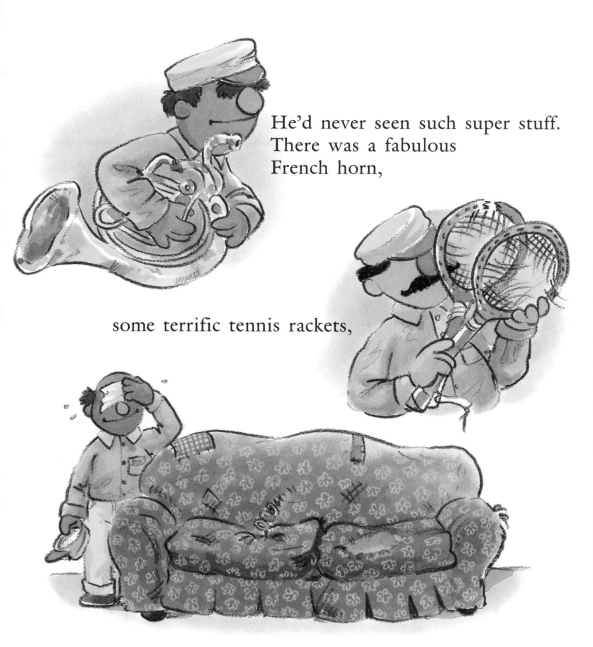

He'd never seen such super stuff.
There was a fabulous
French horn,

some terrific tennis rackets,

and a comfy-looking sofa that was almost
exactly like the one Oscar had.

Then out of the can popped the most gorgeous grouch Oscar had ever seen. She was just about Oscar's size, with snarly pink fur and big googly eyes.

Oscar fell for her like a ton of bricks.

Oscar hurried across the street to introduce himself.

"Hi. I'm Oscar the Grouch," he said in a neighborly way.

"I'm Germaine the Grouch," she said in a grouchy way.

When Oscar heard that, his smile got even broader. "Germaine," he thought to himself. "Germie, for short. What a great name!" Clearly they were made for each other.

But Germaine took one look at Oscar's goofy grin and said, "Get lost, furbrain."

Bright and early the next morning, Oscar
went back to visit his new neighbor. In his
arms he carried a bunch of stinkweeds and a
bag of rotten apples.

Oscar hid the gifts behind his back as he knocked on Germaine's can. He wanted to surprise her. But as soon as Germie saw Oscar, she slammed down the lid. Clang!

Just then, Oscar's friends came walking down
the street.

When Big Bird heard what had happened, he
said, "Gee, Oscar, maybe it's just as well you
didn't give Germaine those presents. I'm pretty
sure girls like roses better than stinkweeds."

"Germie's not a girl," Oscar grumbled. "She's
a grouch!"

"Well, if I were you, I'd get rid of the rotten
apples," Bert suggested helpfully. "I'm sure
she'd rather have candy or something like that."

"Cookies!" added Cookie Monster.

The next day Oscar set off to see Germaine
again. This time he took her a bouquet of red
roses and a two-pound tin of chocolate-chip
cookies.

"Germaine is going to love those flowers,"
said Big Bird.

"And cookies!" said Cookie Monster.

"I just hope you guys know what you're
talking about," Oscar said doubtfully.

"Pee-yew," said Germaine when she saw the
flowers and cookies. "Where'd you get *this* junk,
hairball?" And she told him to get lost again.

"It's all your fault," Oscar growled at Big Bird later that day. "You and those smelly roses."

"Hey, don't blame Big Bird," said Bert. "Maybe if you looked a little neater . . ."

"I think Bert has a point, Oscar," Ernie chimed in. "A bath and a little furcut couldn't hurt. I trim Bert's hair all the time," he said proudly, "and he looks terrific! Why don't you come over to our place and we'll see what we can do with you."

"Promise you won't tell anyone else about
this," Oscar muttered as Ernie combed his fur.
"Relax," said Ernie. "Germaine is going to
love the new you."

But Germaine didn't seem to like the new
Oscar any better than she'd liked the old one.
In other words, not at all.

"Yech! Blech! Aargh!" she cried. "What
happened to *you*, fuzzface?"

And before Oscar could say a word, Germie slammed down her lid again.

As Oscar turned away, he caught sight of his reflection in a store window. For a moment he didn't even recognize himself. He hardly looked like a grouch anymore.

What *had* happened to him? Oscar couldn't help wonder. He'd stopped being himself, that's what! And all to please Germaine.

Suddenly Oscar came to his senses. Grumping
and grumbling, grousing and mumbling, he
stomped off down Sesame Street. By the time
he reached the corner, Oscar the Grouch knew
what he had to do. So he turned around and
stomped back up the street.

Once again Oscar banged on Germie's can,
but this time she wouldn't even come out.

That didn't stop Oscar, though. In his
loudest, grouchiest voice, he proceeded to tell
Germaine exactly what he thought of her.

"You grouchy little grouch . . ." he began.
And ". . . I wouldn't talk to you if you were
the last grouch on earth!" he ended. The
middle part was just too grouchy for words!

Oscar was about to stomp off for the final time when Germaine popped her head out of her can and gave him an irresistibly grouchy grin.

"Now you're talking," she said. "I was beginning to think I was the only true grouch on this whole goody-goody street."

That very afternoon Oscar and Germie had a lovely picnic at the town dump. She brought a basket of sardine-and-jelly sandwiches, he brought a pitcher of lukewarm cabbage-ade, and the two true grouches had a grand old time.